BIGGEST LITTLE MUSTACHE

STARWOOD CHRONICLES, BOOK THREE-SWEET, CLEAN SMALL TOWN ROMANCE

BOBBY HUTCHINSON

SUNFLOWER PUBLISHING

FOREWORD

Deep in the rugged Canadian Rockies, there's this little town called Starwood. Like all small towns, the residents are friendly, mostly kind, curious and helpful.

Like all of us, they have secrets and sometimes unexpected, magical things happen in their lives. And sometimes, bad things as well. I think that's called life.

STARWOOD CHRONICLES

BIGGEST LITTLE TRUCKSTOP
EVERY LITTLE THING
BIGGEST LITTLE MUSTACHE
BIGGEST LITTLE HEART
BIGGEST LITTLE SECRET

1

———

"Bravo-4, to dispatch."

The buzz of radio filled the interior of the marked RCMP vehicle as Constable Chad Montague released the speaker button and waited for a response from the operations control center.

It was three o'clock in the afternoon and his stomach had long since stopped growling. He was beyond hungry, heading for starvation.

Just across the street from where he'd parked Chad could see the Titan, the so-called World's Biggest Truck. The huge monolith was the town of Starwood's claim to fame along with the five coal mines that employed most of the small town's workforce. And not far from the truck was The Biggest Little Truckstop diner where *she* would be waitressing.

He could close his eyes and picture her, thick pink hair cropped short on one side and longer on the other, dipping down over her forehead. She was slender, her shapely figure usually encased in tight jeans and a top that bared a heart-stopping slice of taut midriff. She wore Birkenstocks with bare feet, and toenails painted sometimes purple, sometimes blue. She had a sparkly ankle bracelet that twinkled just under the hem of her jeans.

He'd never seen her in a skirt, but her ankles were fragile and the way the pants fit he just knew she had long, amazing legs. She'd turn around as he walked in, a smile hovering at the corner of her lush lips, her hazel eyes waiting to greet him...

He figured she would do that if only she'd forget about their first meeting when he gave her not one, but *two*, traffic violation tickets. He'd berated himself so many times for that one misguided incident. He'd tried to apologize, but she wouldn't talk to him except to take his food order. Which happened every day, because he couldn't stay away from her.

"*Bravo-four*," the female dispatch operator replied, breaking his daydream.

"It's a ten-twenty-two on the ten-twenty-five call," Chad said, sitting up straight and silently berating himself for getting lost in daydreams while on the job.

"Ten-twenty-two, disregard. There was no burglar. It was Ferguson's foster kid, Marcus. The four-year-old knows how to work the security alarm. Kid's a nightmare, thinks he's a ninja."

A static-filled pause.

Chad knew that whoever was on dispatch was probably laughing in their seat at the control station, thinking he was trying to be funny, but he really wasn't. For some reason, his co-workers either found his deadpan tone and serious face excessively funny or excessively irritating. He couldn't understand why he was so different from them when he was just being professional, being a good officer just like he'd been taught at Depot.

He turned and glanced at himself in the side mirror, wondering what other people saw—what Stella saw--when she looked at him. Dark blonde hair inclined to curl, brown eyes, a square-jawed face, a mustache he was quite proud of. It had been a devil to grow. At barely six feet he was shorter than most of his colleagues, but he made up for it by standing tall.

He figured he might not be much to look at, but he was in top shape. He ran five miles a morning and worked out at the local gym. He could take on either of his taller, older brothers and easily out-wrestle them. As the youngest of three boys, he'd had to learn early to fight. And after his mom died it had been an all-male, no frills household.

"Ten-four, affirmative," the operator finally replied.

"Dispatch," Chad spoke into the car's handheld radio mic, "Bravo-four going on a ten-sixty-two." *Please say yes,* he thought. *Please don't let there be another call.*

Four officers had come down with food poisoning from some backyard barbecue party the other day, a party to which Chad hadn't been invited.

Staff Sergeant Luke Philips was in Vancouver at a conference. With the RCMP for the Elk Valley region already understaffed as it was, all the officers on duty were taking on the extra load today.

"Ten-four. Go have your meal break."

Thank you, thank you! "Ten-four. Thanks, dispatch."

He returned the handheld radio mic to its dashboard mount and popped open the glove compartment, groping around for his Truckstop promo coupon. As he straightened up in his seat, the coupon in his grasp, something made him look up and out through the windshield.

Just across the street, a man in a blue denim shirt with a wrapped bouquet of red and yellow flowers in his arms was looking straight at Chad. The man, a white male, late 30's to mid '40s, about 5'11, brown hair, receding hairline — seemed to have just come from the drugstore and was on his way somewhere.

For a second, Chad met the unknown man's cold stare and his gut twisted as if he'd eaten something bad. Then the crosswalk light changed, and the man crossed the street. *Where had he seen the guy before?*

Chad watched through his side mirror for a second, and then he shook his head at his own paranoia. It wasn't strange for people to stare at cops, and it's not like the man with the flowers was doing anything even remotely suspicious.

Your gut instinct is just telling you it's lunchtime, Constable Chad Montague, he mumbled to himself as he stepped out of the car and strode towards The Truckstop.

Stella Rockley was cleaning out booth number two, putting the dirty dishes and the leftovers—apparently, this customer disliked onions—onto the gray bus pan when she caught a glimpse of the marked police car parked on the other side of the street. She tilted her head, squinting to see which officer it was, but it was too far away to make out the face.

If it was her lucky day, she thought as she sprayed and wiped the table down, Staff Sergeant Luke Philips would be dropping by for hand pies and coffee. He was so charming and friendly, he always brightened her day. He'd married Edna, her boss, Mac Ferguson's sister, a year ago, and Stella loved seeing them together. They were so in love, and now they were expecting a baby any day.

Edna had been in earlier this week, and it looked as if she was ready to pop, although she said it would still be two more weeks.

Stella liked and respected Edna's husband, Luke Philips, because he was genuinely friendly without any intention of hitting on her, unlike a certain constable. Her jaw set when she thought of Constable Montague. She and that up-tight, mustached, miserable excuse for a cop had history, and it made her furious all over again when she remembered.

It was four months ago now, early spring. April 6th, her twenty-fourth birthday.

She'd left Vancouver on impulse. She told people here in Starwood it was because the rent was too high, but really, it was because she felt lost there and alone, despite the fact her mother lived in the city.

Stella had just broken up with her boyfriend. She'd caught him stealing money from her purse to buy drugs, the loser. And Candice, her mother, was on her case again about moving home and pursuing the modelling career Candice had always planned for her daughter.

At 4 am that morning, after a whole long night of lying awake, Stella stared at the crumbling plaster of the ceiling and decided that if she didn't do something she'd grow old alone and rot away in this lonely, rainy city, in this crappy basement apartment, just like that crumbling ceiling.

By 6 am, she'd piled all her stuff in her old beat-up yellow Volkswagen, and shoved an envelope with a note saying she was leaving along with a check for rent owed under her landlady's door.

She phoned in her notice to the restaurant where she waitressed, got in her car and started driving with no idea where she was going. All she knew was that the spring morning was fresh and beautiful, the sky still tinged pink from the dawn, the moon still visible. It was a good day to start over.

She drove all day, singing as she soared over mountain

passes and through valleys still deep in snow. Towards evening, she thought of staying in Fernie, the ski town deep in the Rockies. Her skis were in the rack on top of the car, but the girl she talked to at Starbucks told her that renting even the cheapest of rooms in Fernie would cost more than she could afford, so she drove on.

She was admiring the purple snow-capped mountains and the evergreens that bordered the highway when a flashing light and screaming siren scared her.

The cop car had pulled into place behind her Volkswagen from some side road.

Heart hammering, she pulled over and watched the uniformed police officer step out of his car and walk over. She prayed he wouldn't give her a ticket; she had what was left of her paycheck from waitressing, but it wouldn't go far.

In spite of her fear, Stella noticed how good the officer looked in his uniform, how it showed off his wide shoulders, his trim waist, and his defined arms. When he got to her window, she took one look at his face and felt a little flutter in her stomach.

He looked adorably young for a police officer; face smooth and boyish except for a ridiculous mustache, cheeks flushed pink from the cold. His large, expressive brown eyes were framed by the thickest natural lashes Stella had ever seen. In her modelling days, she'd have killed for natural lashes like that.

She wondered what he'd look like if he smiled. Or if he shaved off what had to be the worst mustache she'd ever laid eyes on.

"Do you know why I pulled you over, ma'am?" he said, his thick brows pulling down into a little frown.

"No officer," she said. "I have no idea. I know I wasn't speeding."

"Your signal lights at the back are broken," he said. "Did you know about that?"

"I didn't know," she said. "Or I would have used hand signals on that lane change."

"Well," the young officer rested his hands on his belt and shifted his feet. He looked around at the highway, squinting into the growing dusk. "Fix them as soon as you get into town. Starwood's only five minutes that way." He pointed in the direction she'd been going.

"I was sort of planning on driving into Alberta before stopping for the—"

The Starbucks girl had given her the phone number of a youth hostel in Coleman, the small Alberta town just past the border of B.C.

"Well, I'm telling you," he cut her off, "you need to stop in Starwood and get them fixed as soon as possible. Hand signals are for emergencies only."

"Alright," she said with a dejected shrug of her shoulders. "Is there a garage there that could fix them for me tonight?"

"The Esso will be open, but whether they'll have parts for a Volkswagen I couldn't say."

"Okay, I'll try them." She was more than a little annoyed at how bossy he was, but it was easy to forgive a cute guy, and he *was* just doing his job to keep everyone safe on the road.

"Thank you. I appreciate your advice. I'm not from around here, so I wouldn't know where to get this fixed or which mechanic I could trust not to try and cheat me, you know?"

He blinked his long lashes at her like he had no idea where she was going with this or why she was wasting his time with things that had nothing to do with him.

She wondered if she could make him smile or even laugh. Playfully, she gave him her most appealing look, the look that always brought guys to their knees. *What the heck, it was her birthday.*

"I'll have to stay in Starwood tonight. If you were to give me your name and phone number," she purred, remembering too late that she hadn't looked in a mirror all day, "I could maybe ask you for advice on where to stay, or what's the best place to eat? Things like that."

He stared at her, his expression growing cold and stiff. "The name is Constable Chad Montague, RCMP, Starwood Detachment. The *number* is subsection one-seven-one, parenthesis two of the Motor Vehicle Act. Your violation for driving without a signal device will cost you a fine of $109 and two points off your driving record."

"What?" she said, in shock.

"I need you to produce your driver's license and insurance, please."

"But I thought you were letting me go?" she said, her voice rising in panic.

"You were in clear violation of a driving law, and you were trying to weasel your way out of it by brown-nosing me. You're getting slapped with a ticket, ma'am."

"I wasn't. . ." She felt her face grow hot with embarrassment. Actually, she was.

"I just wanted to. . ." She couldn't bring herself to say it, that she'd actually, genuinely wanted to get his number, that she'd thought he was really cute and maybe they could get to know each other. It was humiliating. She swallowed hard, on the verge of tears.

And it went downhill from there when she couldn't find her insurance papers or her driver's license.

"I just piled my whole life into my car this morning on a whim," she told him, frantically delving through the detritus of her life, her voice wobbling. "My purse *has* to be here somewhere, I had it when I got gas a while back." A long while back, she remembered. "Maybe it's in the backseat under some of those boxes?" She opened the car door to get out and see.

"Stay in your vehicle, ma'am."

He stared at her coldly and slapped her with *another* ticket for failing to produce a driver's license or insurance, and an additional $81 fine.

It would take almost every last cent of her money. She'd have to sleep in the car and try and find work in Starwood first thing in the morning. The gas gauge on the car was registering barely a quarter of a tank.

By the time she drove off, she was cursing Constable Montague under her breath, and it was all she could do not to flip him the finger as she made her left-turn hand signal and drove carefully into town.

As she carried loads of dishes into the kitchen, Stella remembered again exactly how terrified she'd felt that night. The Esso station was open, but there was no mechanic available until morning. She'd parked in the hotel parking lot, locked the doors and barely closed her eyes all night, afraid that the nasty cop would write her yet another ticket for sleeping in a public place or something else ridiculous. What a way to spend her birthday.

She'd had her first bit of good luck the following morning. There was a sign in the window of the Biggest Little Truckstop when she stumbled in for coffee.

Waitress Wanted.

She'd cleaned up in the washroom, applied for the job and been hired on the spot. She'd worked here ever since.

The small town had welcomed her, she'd found a lovely affordable room at the local B&B.

The only fly in the ointment was Constable Montague. Of course, he ate at the Truckstop, everyone did. She gritted her teeth against the urge to spit in his meal whenever he came in.

Out of the corner of her eye, she spied movement by booth five. She turned and sure enough, the tourist family of three (with the charming British accents) had just finished their meal. The brunette lady in a messy bun and a paisley blouse, whom Stella assumed to be the mother of the two boys, was looking in Stella's direction, her hand partially raised, as if she needed the washroom.

Stella grinned and headed over. "Would you like to order some dessert?"

"Oh," the lady said, as if she'd been startled by the suggestion, "well, Miss, I was just about to ask for the bill but--"

The door flew open with a sudden startling bang and the bell attached to the top jangled violently.

"Oh, bugger!" The tourist lady spilled her water.

As Stella mopped it up, she sensed that everyone had stopped eating to look. She glanced over her shoulder and there, standing in the doorway was Montague, soldier straight, square-jawed, tanned red-brown from the sun and, as usual, sporting that most distasteful but most well-groomed mustache.

She loved the fact that it looked awful on him.

So it was her *unlucky* day. If there was one cop below forty that Stella didn't find somewhat attractive, it was Montague. She told herself that not even the smart uniform and the physically fit body could ever change her first opinion.

"Ooooooh, a copper," mumbled one of the boys, craning their neck to look.

"Is someone going to get arrested, mummie?" the other boy said in a mock whisper.

"Psst!" said a voice by the kitchen area.

Stella turned to find Jamie leaning out the pass-thru.

It's GI Joe, he mouthed at her, moving his lips slowly, syllable by syllable.

Stella rolled her eyes at him. Jamie knew how she felt about Montague, and he delighted in teasing her. It irritated her no end. And for some unknown reason, she also hated having Jamie make fun of Montague.

"Ahem!" Montague coughed into his fist, the door closing slowly behind him, much less violently than it had been opened. He raised a hand, gave a ridiculous little wave and nodded his head at the people in the diner.

Was that supposed to be an apology for disturbing the peace? Stella shook her head and turned back to her customers. *He can't even open his mouth to say sorry for slamming the door and scaring the lights out of everyone?*

Stella smiled at the British tourists. "Sorry about that. Did you say you'd like to order dessert?"

"Oh, may we have pudding, please mummie?" The younger boy with the blue eyes and freckles bounced up and down on his seat.

"We need to go soon, darling." The woman was still eyeing Montague with some trepidation.

"How about I pack up a dessert of your choice," suggested Stella, "and you can eat it along the way?"

"Oh well, Miss, that sounds a good idea—"

"Ahem," Constable Montague coughed loudly into his fist again. He was still standing in the middle of the diner, just inside the doorway.

Stella ignored him. "Hold on, I'll get you the dessert menu." She hurried off to get one.

On the way, she passed by Montague. She leaned in slightly towards him and hissed, "Unless it's a matter of life and death, please take a seat like other normal human people and *stop scaring my customers.*"

He stiffened up even straighter, his face turning magenta.

Stella felt both mean and pleased at having embarrassed him.

"Not on police business," he grumbled in that low, gravelly voice of his, staring straight ahead at some point just above Stella's head, "I'm just here to order."

"Well, then you don't need to stand there like a statue, do you?" Stella said in a low, venomous tone. "Go pick a seat."

Montague shifted from foot to foot for a second, and then he pivoted on his heel and made straight for one of the booths.

As Stella went by to grab the dessert menu, Jamie poked his head out the pass-thru and grinned. He was wearing his battered Stetson as usual. Stella called him the cowboy cook. He whispered, "Did you suggest something dirty to him? And if so, what?"

"I simply told him to take a seat."

"That's not what it looked like," said Jamie. "I swear, you've got the hots for GI Joe. And vice versa."

"Get back in the kitchen where you belong, you pervert."

"His ears are *still* red," Jamie said, looking over to the small, two-person table where Constable Montague had settled. "Man, you really like those uniforms. Coming on to mustache man, of all people."

"I was *not* flirting with him!"

"Nope," Jamie said. "You were totally *seducing* him! Look at the poor guy, he can barely sit still. GI Joe's in love with you, Stella baby."

"I have customers waiting. And so do you!" Stella stomped away towards booth five with the menu. She could hear Jamie chortling.

"What would you suggest, Miss?" The British brigade were all still casting sidelong glances at Montague.

"Pick and Shovel Pie. It's chocolate and caramel in a nutty almond crust. Or Coal Miner Cookies, they're walnut and chocolate chip."

"Biscuits, mummie, please. May we each have a biscuit?"

Mummie ordered four cookies, and Stella went to pack them up in a cardboard coal miner's lunch box. They were delighted, and Stella got a generous tip when they paid their bill and left.

By the time she made her way over to Montague, two more customers had come in and sat down. She threw them a smile as she drew out her pad and took down the pencil she'd stuck behind her ear. She scowled when Montague didn't look up from the menu. He'd certainly had enough time to make a decision while she attended to the tourist mother and her kids. He was probably winding her up.

"Are you ready to order, officer?" Her voice was haughty.

"Ummmm," he said. "Yeah. I'll uh. . . I'll have whatever you'd recommend, Stella." He looked up at her then, and she couldn't help but stare at his mustache.

God, it's so tacky. It's so awful. What ever made him think he'd look good with a mustache?

"What did you say?" He blinked in surprise at her.

She tore her gaze from his mustache and met his brown eyes. *Did I say that out loud?* In the light from the window, his irises were almost a pale honey, and his lashes were thick and full, fanning out from his lids like falsies—the models she once knew would kill to have natural lashes like those.

"Mousse," she said. "We're. . . uh. . . having blueberry cheesecake mousse next week. On the dessert menu. New product." *No, we're not. Jamie's gonna kill me. But hey, it actually sounds yummy.*

"Oh," he said. "I don't want dessert. I'm just here for lunch."

"I know that," said Stella with a lift of her chin and a toss of her hair. "How about the coal miner's lunch? Isn't that what you usually have?"

"Right. Okay. I'll have that, then," As he said it, his mustache twitched. "And Stella?"

She clutched her notepad and stiffened her spine, preparing for some nasty comment. He'd pissed off lots of the locals. Edna Ferguson called him *that miserable excuse for a Mountie.*

Jamie called him *GI Joe.*

Luke just called him *young and overzealous.*

Stella personally thought he was plain old arrogant and superior; even his swaggering body language showed he had an over-inflated male ego. But it wasn't kind of people to make fun of him, either.

His brows furrowed and his mustache twitched again, then a corner of his mouth lifted, or at least she thought it did. She couldn't quite see his mouth under that thick mustache.

Is that a smirk? Is he making fun of me? Trying to intimidate me?

She turned away and bellowed, "One Coal Miner's lunch for the constable, Jamie."

The smile hadn't worked.

Dejected, Chad rested his forearms on the table,

absently fiddling with the brim of his hat, caressing the smoothness of the black, shiny plastic. If anything she'd gotten more hostile the moment he'd tried to smile at her. She was never going to give him a second look. He'd blown it with her right in the beginning.

If only he was better with people. With *women*. Well, not women in general. Just better with Stella. He's seen the way she smiled at Staff.

Chad knew he was nothing like Staff Sergeant Luke Philips who was tall, handsome, friendly and seemed to always know exactly the right thing to say.

Nope, he'd been born awkward and tongue-tied, although he'd been top of his class at Depot and valedictorian at his high school. He could have gone to the University of BC with a full scholarship, but he didn't want to wait four years before following in his father's and his older brother's footsteps and putting on the RCMP uniform.

He was proud of who he was and what he had achieved up to this point. He was good at sports, especially soccer; he was good at academics; he was good at everything except interpersonal skills.

He so wanted Stella to look at him like she was happy to see him. He watched her flitting from one table to the next, smiling, joking, laughing.

She was so beautiful. Stylishly cut hair, barely an inch long on one side and cropped to a few inches below her jawline on the other, so it swung forward and emphasized her high cheekbones. It was dyed in several shades of pink. She had huge almond-shaped dark blue eyes and that lean, long-limbed figure that he tried not to stare at.

Chad looked down at the hat in his hands. The brim was matted with his fingerprints. He'd always gotten in trouble at the Depot for this habit. *Stop fondling your hat, cadet!* his superior officer used to shout. *Or I'll make you polish every single hat at the Requisitions Office until you can see your own face in it!*

Chad shook his head. Those were the days. He grabbed a table napkin from the dispenser and tried to wipe off the prints but ended up with very visible pieces of white napkin fibre stuck to the black brim of his officer's hat.

"One order of Coal Miner's Lunch," Stella said, her voice approaching quickly from behind him.

Chad jolted and turned, dropping his hat on the table.

Stella moved the hat and set the plate down in front of him, arranging it so the cherry tomato salad was on his left, the large slab of pastry-coated vegetables and meat on the upper right corner, and the seasoned potato wedges on the lower right side.

The heady aroma of the beef stew filling wafted up to him, mixed with the golden smell of the kind of lard-shortened pie crust Chad's mother used to make when he was a little kid. His mouth was starting to really water just looking at it.

"You're welcome," Stella snapped.

Chad looked up from his food, his mouth opening to apologize, but she had already turned her attention to the next customer two tables over.

It's not a big deal, he thought to himself, picking up his fork. *People sometimes forget to say thank you in situations like this all the time, don't they?*

He ate one bite of the pie, and it was pretty close to heaven. The second forkful was halfway to his mouth when the radio clipped to his vest crackled.

"Bravo-four, there's a ten-twenty-five in progress at the Ferguson's farm."

Chad put down his fork with reluctance. Another

burglar alarm at the same address? All within the last two hours?

He'd bet it was that wild little ninja kid again, climbing and crawling into places he shouldn't be and setting off the alarms.

It was brave of Mac Ferguson and his wife Kate to take the kid on. Chad had heard that some relative of Kate's had died back east. The story was she was a single parent, and there were no other relatives, so Kate and Mac took the boy.

Chad had told the kid just an hour ago in no uncertain terms that he was absolutely not allowed to fool around with the alarm, but that was obviously a waste of breath.

Or maybe it was Mac and Edna's mother, Dixie Ferguson, the elderly lady with Alzheimer's. She'd maybe set it off. She'd done that several times in the last month.

She was now living in the care home in Starwood, but her family often brought her to the farm for visits. He hadn't seen her today when he attended the last call, but that didn't mean she wasn't at the farm.

Mac and Kate were out of town for the week for some kind of meeting with an important investor, or so Chad had overheard from the grapevine. They'd left their two kids with Edna and Luke.

The whole family lived in the old Ferguson place, Edna and Staff Sergeant Philips in the old farmhouse, Mac and Kate in a new house Mac had built, and they all switched off caring for Dixie when she was visiting.

"Bravo-four, do you copy? There's a ten-twenty-five at the Ferguson's farm again. No other units available."

Chad sighed. There went his lunch break.

"Ten-four," he replied, standing up and placing his fingerprint-smudged cap snugly back onto his head. "Bravo-four, ten-seventeen. I'm on my way."

Movement from the corner of his eye made him turn. It was Stella walking up to his table with a plastic bag and an empty take-out container. She quickly dumped all the food from his plate into the container, the pie mixing with the tomato salad and the tomato salad mixing with the potato wedges.

For a dumbfounded moment, he watched her nimble fingers pack the take-out container into the plastic bag, drop a plastic knife and fork in, and, at lightning speed, knot the handles of the bag. She pushed the plastic bag into his hand.

"Go, go, go!" Stella said. He felt her hand tap his vest just above his heart. Later on, he'd wonder if she'd meant to tap him on the shoulder for good luck and aborted the action mid-way, or if she'd meant to push him out the door fast.

"Right. Thank you." Chad pivoted on his heel and jogged out to his car.

He didn't use the siren for the twelve minutes it took to drive the Elk Valley road, but he did travel at speed. When he turned into the driveway the first thing he saw was a black Volvo.

No one at the farm drove a black Volvo, he was sure of that. And the car hadn't been there when he was here before.

Then a crash and the sound of glass breaking, plus a kid screaming, came from inside the house, and he jumped out of the patrol car and raced up the porch steps.

2

———

Four-year-old Marcus tried not to breathe too loudly as he tucked in his feet and huddled deeper into the shadows under the corner table.

The tasseled end of the table runner dangled in front of his face, the tassels still swinging from when he'd brushed past it and crawled here to hide from the bad man.

Marcus was kinda good at playing hide-and-seek, but this time, it wasn't Uncle Mac or Auntie Kate or his cousin Susie, or even Aunt Edna or Uncle Luke he was hiding from. This time he couldn't get found. Something bad would happen if he got found. He could feel his heart hammering against his Superman tee shirt.

"Little *Kaaaty-boy*," the bad man called in a soft sing-song voice. His boots thumped along the wooden floor in the hallway. "I heard Kate's not here. But one little chick *is*, and the other will be home soon. So Kate'll be here pretty quick, won't she? To be with her chickees. And then we'll have a talk, her and I."

The bad man's voice was different from Uncle Mac's, or from the mustache-policeman's low, robo-cop tone.

Marcus didn't like the bad man. He'd kicked Pansy, Auntie Edna's newest puppy. Pansy had run away yelping.

Marcus knew he'd been very naughty.

Auntie Kate and Auntie Edna had told him time and again he wasn't to open the front door when the bell rang, not unless an adult was with him. But he'd thought maybe it was mommy come to get him at last, so he'd unlocked it and yanked it open.

They kept saying his mommy was in some place called Heaven, but Marcus knew she'd come for him as soon as she could.

But the bad man with the flowers had pushed the door hard and come in. And Pansy had barked and growled at him, and then she'd bit his ankle. The man kicked her and said a bad word, and he didn't even close the door behind him the way you were supposed to.

"Well, little boy, where's your auntie? I know she's around here somewhere."

His voice was low, but his eyes and his face were mean. He dropped the flowers on the floor and reached for Marcus.

Quick as the snake in his favorite cartoon, Marcus slithered out of the man's reach and quickly stretched up and pushed the alarm on the wall the way Uncle Luke had taught him, and then he'd run as fast as he could, through the hall and into the living room.

He'd already gotten in trouble with Auntie for pushing the alarm earlier today, but Uncle Luke and Uncle Mac had told him lots of times, "If something happens that scares you, if there's a fire or somebody's hurt, you push the alarm hard."

The first time he'd pushed it today he'd thought maybe it would make his mommy come for him. Instead, he'd gotten in trouble with Auntie and with the mustache policeman. He'd promised not to do it again, but this man with the mean face really scared him.

He wished hard that Auntie Edna would come in the house. She'd know what to do about the bad man. She'd gone out to the barn with the dogs to feed the horses.

He was supposed to stay close to her, but he'd wanted a cookie, so he and Pansy sneaked back inside. Auntie was gonna be really, really mad at him for not doing as he was told. He didn't care as long as she came in and made the bad man leave.

The slow *thump, thump* of the boots became a muffled *thud, thud, thud* as the bad man came into the living room where Marcus was hiding. He walked around and then stopped right in front of the corner table. "Found you, little chick."

Marcus stared at the boots. There was a reason Susie often shouted "*you little cheater*" at Marcus whenever they played any games. Marcus could really cheat if he wanted to; unless someone made him feel bad about it. But against the bad man, he wouldn't feel bad at all.

Marcus darted out from under the table, fast like a rabbit from its hole. He grabbed at the tassels and pulled the table runner with him as he went. The bad man's hand swiped at the air, barely missing Marcus. Auntie's huge vase of flowers sitting on top of the table runner came crashing down.

The bad man screamed at him. He was really, really mad, but Marcus didn't look back. He just ran for the front door.

But the door flew open just as Marcus got near. And there in the doorway stood mustache-policeman, one hand on the gun at his belt. His eyes were wide, and he looked a little scared as he stared down at Marcus.

"You okay, kid?" he said in a rush. He didn't quite sound like robo-cop anymore, but he still looked a bit like one, the way he stood all stiff.

"*YOU ROTTEN LITTLE DEMON SPAWN!*" the bad man screamed, stumbling out from the living room.

Marcus glimpsed something in his hand. It looked like one of the toy guns his mommy wouldn't ever buy for him. She'd said guns were weapons that only policemen should have. Uncle Luke and the mustache policeman had one.

Mustache policeman drew his gun out now really fast and pointed it at the bad man.

"Quick kid," he said to Marcus, suddenly calm and robot-like again, not taking his eyes off the bad man for even a second. "Scoot behind me, then run fast outside and hide, okay?"

Marcus didn't hesitate. He squeezed past the policeman, who stood blocking the doorway, his gun trained on the bad man.

Marcus' head bumped the policeman's elbow as was easing by. The gun jerked.

"*Gotcha!*" the bad man shouted, and then *bang*.

So loud. And again *bang*.

Policeman dropped to his knees, his arm blocking Marcus from the bad man.

Marcus could feel the policeman shaking as he pressed something square and flat into Marcus' hands. "Run, run and hide," he said. "When you're safe, call 911. Tell them—"

Another *bang* and part of the door jamb exploded into splinters. The policeman shoved Marcus through the doorway, hard enough to make Marcus stumble and fall on his butt on the welcome mat, and the policeman slammed the door shut in his face.

Marcus scrambled up, sobbing. From the other side of the door, he could hear more gunshots and heavy thumps. Shouting.

Marcus looked down at the cell phone the policeman gave him and ran, the phone clutched in his hands, around the house towards the barn, screaming for Auntie Edna.

She must have heard him because she came tearing around the corner of the house and caught him in her arms, and he gabbled out what the policeman had said.

"911, policeman said push 911," Marcus kept hollering. "He gots a gun, the bad man gots a gun. They both has guns."

Auntie Edna pushed the buttons and then she ran fast, carrying Marcus tight in her arms, talking on the phone in a high, jerky voice as she ran.

Her belly with the baby in it made a shelf for Marcus to rest his bum, and he wrapped his arms and legs around his auntie and wailed into her shoulder.

3

———————

Chad blinked hard, trying to stay awake even as he kept one hand pressed to his neck where the bullet had grazed. Warm, sticky blood seeped through his fingers and ran down his forearm. Breathing was painful; his chest hurt. Thank god for the soft body armor; he'd likely have been dead without it.

If only he could call for help or backup.

The radio clipped to his vest was the first thing the perp had hit. Then Chad had taken the shot right near his heart. It had brought him to his knees, stunned. He'd felt the blunt impact force of the bullet on his vest. Thank god, he'd managed to get the kid out of harm's way, shoved his cell at him.

Maybe Marcus had actually been able to call for help.....

Where was the shooter? Anxious now, he turned his head, searching. Slumped across from him on the floor, the man stared glassy-eyed at nothing. Dead.

Chad's eyelids fluttered down. He was so tired. His limbs felt like jelly. He'd just had his first violent confrontation with a perp. He'd killed him. His co-workers couldn't call him a rookie anymore. Maybe he could rest for a bit.....

He didn't know when he'd closed his eyes, but in the darkness of half-sleep, he thought he felt a soft tapping on his vest, just over his heart. It was bruised there; it should hurt, but it didn't. It was Stella, telling him go, go, go.....

Chad blinked awake, looking for her, but she wasn't there.

Pain shot through him. And then darkness.

Chad woke up to the steady beeping of his heart monitor, the drip, drip of the IV bag above him, clean sheets that smelled like bleach, white walls, and the flash of evening sunlight behind green curtains. He knew hospitals like the back of his hand, and he hated them.

A third of his early life was spent hanging around hospitals, visiting his mother while she fought against her recurring cancer again and again. He remembered her proud smile when he came to her hospital room one day and told her he was going to be a policeman like his dad.

He remembered the white shroud being pulled over her face.

As a patrol officer, he'd brought people to hospitals on almost a daily basis, injured, drunk, overdosed, or suicidal.

He'd stood beside hospital beds a lot, even as a rookie officer, taking statements from victims and witnesses hooked up to IV drips and heart monitors, and sometimes even a respirator. He never got used to them.

Now it was his turn to lie on the bed, more than a little high on the meds, feeling unmoored and lost, like some kid's birthday balloon that they'd forgotten to tie down to the back of a chair or a post.

A touch on his hand made him look down at the slender

fingers covering his own. He followed the arm attached to the hand, all the way up to the smiling face, the pink hair, and the deep blue almond-shaped eyes of Stella Rockley.

"Oh, it's you," he said, feeling something like awe as he looked at her.

"Yup, it's me, surprise, surprise," she said, her face soft and her smile real.

"What are you doing here?" he said. "You're smiling at me. You never smile at me."

"Is it a violation, officer?" she said, still smiling. "Are you going to fine me?"

He was too drugged out to say anything but the truth. "I thought you hated me."

"I don't hate you," she said, faltering. "Well, maybe I did before, but not now....." she trailed off.

"You embarrassed me. Back when we first met, that night you gave me those tickets. I actually...." she paused again. "I actually was trying to get you to ask me out."

"I actually," he echoed, "have never met anyone like you." The drugs were making his tongue say things he'd never have had the courage to say. "You're beautiful and smart and sexy, and I think I'm in love with you---"

"Uh-huh," she said, with a wry twist of her mouth. "And you're high as a kite."

"I'm in heaven?"

"No," she laughed, sounding like morning sunshine and cool summer rain all at once. "Heaven doesn't allow mustaches. You have to shave it off."

"Yeah?" he said. "Okay. Mom might not recognize me in heaven with the mustache anyway."

"Your mother?" she said, squeezing his hand.

"She—she died. She had cancer."

"I'm so sorry. How old were you?"

"Fifteen."

"That must have been tough."

"Yeah." He closed his eyes, hoping the tears that threatened didn't leak out. He was so tired....

"Your number," he said, just as the thought came to him, "put it in my phone, so we can call each other. Please?" He turned his hand under her palm and wove his fingers between hers.

Stella stared down at their linked hands, then back up at him. "I think they might have overdosed you. Let me check with the nurse."

Chad felt an impulse to kiss the back of her hand. He didn't think twice. He brought her hand to his mouth and planted a kiss. She instantly pulled her hand away like she'd been stung.

"Stella Rockley," he slurred. "You're under arrest for grand larceny. You've stolen my heart."

She sighed. "I don't know why I'm not finding this funny right now, because your behavior is absolutely hilarious, Constable Uptight."

"You stole my heart, so you better give me your number," he murmured, sinking back into his pillows, feeling suddenly tired. "Where's my phone? I need to phone you."

"It's with Marcus, I think." Stella had a strange expression on her face.

Chad didn't think he'd ever seen her look like that. "I'll go get it for you." She got up so fast her chair crashed to the floor. "They brought him in to check him over, but he's not hurt."

"And my lunch," he added as she moved to leave the room. "The pick-and-shovel pie you packed for me. I left it in.....the.....car....."

Chad's lids grew heavy, and with a sigh he let sleep wash over him.

The last thing he saw was Stella's shadow, her long limbs and graceful form outlined in the doorway as she turned to look back at him.

4

"Are you back with us now, Constable?"

Chad blinked awake.

His NCO, Staff Sergeant Luke Philips, was lounging in the chair next to his bed, tall boots propped on the bedside table. He was in red serge, and he looked impressive. He also looked tired.

It must be late at night, the hospital sounded hushed and the partially drawn window curtains showed a sliver of darkness.

"Hello sir," Chad croaked, hand flying up to rub at his throat. His fingers met the distinct texture of hospital gauze and medical tape instead. "*Owww.*"

"Bullet grazed you," his superior officer said. "A little bit more to the left and you'd be dead."

"The little boy, Marcus—"

"He's fine. He's with my wife."

Chad heaved a sigh of relief. "The man I shot—he died at the scene." Chad shuddered, remembering.

"Sure did. And good riddance. He was positively ID'd as Jack Ames."

It took a moment for the name to register. "That stalker, the Calgary guy. I *knew* I'd seen his photo somewhere."

Ames had stalked Mac's wife, Kate, in Calgary before she'd moved here and married Mac.

He'd also even made an appearance at Staff's wedding when he was marrying Mac's sister Edna. That night, Staff had made certain all the RCMP personnel knew about Ames. They'd kept a sharp eye out for him for months, but he'd stayed in Calgary. There had been another report of him stalking a woman there, but nothing recent.

"Apparently he sexually assaulted a woman in Calgary the night before last, and nearly killed her. Then he stole a car, a black Volvo, and drove here. He talked to one of the young girls at the drugstore, Sandra Davies, and she told him all about Kate and Mac taking on Marcus, how wonderful everyone thinks that is."

He snorted. "Small towns, everyone knows what color underwear people have on. Anyway, Sandra didn't know they were away. She gave him directions up to the farm. She feels terrible about it, but it probably won't stop her from gossiping. You remember Ames turned up at Mac's wedding?"

"Yeah, I heard about it. It happened on my first shift here."

Chad had just been transferred to Starwood that week, and he'd stopped Edna for driving erratically that afternoon. She was searching for her mother, Dixie Ferguson.

Dixie had wandered away from Mac's wedding. Chad had had Edna's car towed that afternoon. He was pretty sure she still despised him for that.

God, he made so many mistakes with people.

It was such a relief to hear that the little ninja kid was okay. But something else bothered Chad. Something that wasn't in his NCO's succinct briefing made him feel guilty and troubled.

"I was stupid, sir," Chad said finally, struggling to sit up on the bed.

"Stay down, Montague," Sergeant Philips said, putting his booted feet back down on the ground and gesturing for Chad to lie back.

Chad ignored him. "I should have avoided direct conflict and taken the kid with me to the car and then called for backup. Instead, I locked myself in with the perp and left the kid to run off on his own."

"I've heard Marcus' story," said Philips. "The boy was pretty clear about all that went down. I think you made as good a call as you could have in that situation, considering that you'd already been shot."

He put a hand on Chad's shoulder and looked Chad straight in the eye. "There'll be an internal investigation, that's standard when there's a shooting, but yours was totally justified. I'm proud of you, Constable. Your father and brothers are proud of you too. They've all been notified of your actions, and they'll be in touch, probably tomorrow. My family owes you a huge debt of gratitude. You saved Marcus's life, and probably Edna's as well."

Staff swallowed hard and cleared his throat when he mentioned his wife. "Thank you."

Chad gulped and looked away, more than a little uncomfortable. He had no idea what to say to that. *Your welcome* wasn't quite right.

"Just doing my job, sir. Like I was trained to do," he said. But his voice wasn't as controlled as usual. It quavered, and he, too, cleared his throat, feeling himself get hot and red.

Luke Philips smiled at him, his cheeks dimpling and black curls flopping into his eyes. Chad briefly remembered all the times he'd seen Stella respond to that smile and the signature Luke Philips charm that went with it.

This was the kind of guy Stella was attracted to, not a boring, straight-laced cop like Chad. His heart sank. Even though he thought she'd said that the time he pulled her over, she was actually trying to flirt with him.

Or had he imagined her saying that? He'd been pretty groggy. He must have imagined it. She'd never flirt with someone like him, a beautiful woman like Stella.

"Get some rest," said Philips, patting Chad's arm. "I want a full report as soon as you're somewhat recovered. I'll send one of the boys over with a laptop."

"Yes, sir," he said.

"And don't forget to give her a callback," Philips said, pointing to the bedside table where Chad's phone sat next to a huge vase of sunflowers and various get-well cards from the precinct. "Your girlfriend's been calling, probably hoping you've woken up already."

Chad just stared at the phone, and then back at his boss. "What girlfriend, sir?" Chad didn't have a girlfriend.

"Stella. She's pretty shaken up by all this," said Philips, getting up from his chair and brushing invisible dust from his shoulder insignia. "The medics told her you'd lost a dangerous amount of blood." He paused on his way out the door and shook his head. "She came straight to the hospital when she heard. She was pretty upset. She's a real pretty girl, Montague. Nice, too. You're a lucky man."

"What are you talking about, sir?" Chad finally managed to say, but Staff Sergeant Philips had already shut the door behind himself and didn't hear a word he'd said.

Chad looked over at his bedside table where the cell phone sat innocently beside the vase of sunflowers, half-buried under the get-well cards. Pain flared over his chest and all over his neck as he leaned over and stretched out his arm to grab it—the same phone he had placed in Marcus's hands as he'd told him to run away and call for help.

The screen said he had six missed calls. Two were from —Stella.

He smoothed his finger over the screen. Should he call her back?

He touched the first number and then deleted it.

She probably just felt sorry for him. People in Starwood were like that, they empathized when someone was hurt.

He wouldn't bother her.

5

———

Stella wiped the dishcloth around the inside of the glass, her mind far away in a hospital room. *You stole my heart, so you better give me your number.*

What did that mean? What did he mean by it?

It had been more than a week since she'd last seen him in the hospital, but she still couldn't stop thinking about it. If he was doped up when he said it, did that make his words more honest, or did that make it just a bunch of random nonsense? And why hadn't he called her?

If any other young, single guy had said those things to her and kissed her hand like that, Stella would obviously have taken it as an expression of romantic interest.

But this was Constable Chad Montague, the same guy who'd brutally shut her down when she'd tried to get his number, slapping her with tickets and fines and accusing her of trying to weasel her way out of trouble.

Stella turned the drinking glass round and round in her hands, the dishcloth making squeaking noises against the outside of the glass.

She remembered the open, vulnerable expression on his

face as he lay there, bandages wrapped around his neck, looking at her like she was the only thing in his world.

The man in that hospital bed didn't seem like the same man Stella had labelled as a cold, arrogant, self-centered idiot all these months.

How and when had she begun to think of him in such a bad light? Was it.....was it just because he'd made a terrible first impression on her? Because he'd embarrassed and humiliated her when she had been at her weakest and reached out to him, hoping for.....

"Stella, my lady." Jamie poked his head out the pass-thru. "How long are you going to polish that one drinking glass? You've been doing that for practically an hour already. Even glass wears down, y'know."

Stella glanced at the clock and quickly put the drinking glass away. "It wasn't an hour," she said.

"Ha," said Jamie as he puttered around in the kitchen. "Keep telling yourself that. When are you going to admit that you and GI Joe are a matched set?"

The little bell attached to the front door tinkled. Stella turned around, already gathering two menus from the counter. "Welcome to The Truckstop—"

She lost her breath.

It was him. He was in civilian clothes: casual jeans, a white t-shirt stretched across an impressive chest, a plaid, flannel button-down he wore open and untucked.

And omigosh, omigod, his face was clean-shaven. He looked entirely different without the mustache, younger, more vulnerable. Handsome as hell.

"It's gone," she said, walking up to him and staring at his upper lip where the mustache used to be. He had great lips. He had a sexy mouth. Who knew?

He cleared his throat and lifted up a hand to cover his

mouth self-consciously. "Yeah. I uh, I got rid of it," he said, deliberately putting his hand down and then awkwardly rubbing the back of his neck. "I seem to remember you telling me it had to go."

"You look—wow, you look so.....different."

"Better different, I hope?" He sounded insecure.

"*Much* better. When did you get out of the hospital?"

She'd been going to go and visit him again, but she'd gotten nervous about it. He hadn't returned her calls, and he'd probably be totally embarrassed if she reminded him of the things he'd said.

"Just this morning. I'm sorry I didn't call you back all week. I just thought it'd be better if I could stop by in person."

Stella noticed that his ears had turned pink. She nodded her head and said, "I see," for lack of anything else to say.

"Actually," he added, out of the blue, "I had this funny dream that my mom—well, that I was about to get into heaven, but I got turned back because they didn't allow people with mustaches to go in." He was totally deadpan, which made his words even funnier.

Stella giggled. She couldn't help it.

"In the hospital, you said your mom wouldn't know you with the mustache. In Heaven," she added. "Remember?"

"I did? I don't remember saying that."

Stella blinked, thinking of their talk in the hospital room. Did he remember what he'd said about being in love with her?

Probably not. Here she was, obsessing over what they'd said to each other in the hospital room, and he'd pretty much forgotten it all.

He nodded, and then there was a long silence until he straightened and stood bolt upright.

For a crazy moment, she thought he was going to salute.

"I know you're working, Stella, so I won't take up too much of your time."

That's all he has to say? Stella thought. *He's leaving now?*

"Officer," she called out to him.

He paused halfway to the front door and turned around. "Call me Chad, please." He gestured down to his clothes. "Especially since I'm out of uniform and all."

"When I went to visit you at the hospital—" she trailed off, searching his face for any sign that he remembered.

"Yes?" he said, his brown eyes lighting up, a hopeful expression on his face.

"Nothing," she said, forcing herself to smile. "I just wanted to say that---that I'm glad you're okay now."

He nodded again and tipped an invisible hat at her. Then he pivoted on his heel and was out the door.

Stella stared after him with a slow, sinking feeling in her gut.

"I thought this was supposed to be a happy meeting," Jamie said, coming up behind her to watch Chad Montague drive off. "But the two of you look like an ex-couple forced to meet again to sign divorce papers."

"There's no *two of us*, Jamie."

"Exactly," he said. "And I keep telling you there should be. Get over yourself and give the guy a break, Stella-mia."

6

C had felt like kicking himself as he drove to the police station to pick up some stuff from his locker. He was on paid leave for a month, and he planned to spend part of each day at the gym, working out so he stayed in shape.

What *was* that back there at the diner? He'd rehearsed what he'd say to her and imagined all the possible scenarios but the moment he walked in and saw her, the moment he met her eyes, he forgot everything he'd planned to say. He was just hopelessly awkward at talking to people. Face it, he was hopeless period with women. With Stella.

As a police officer, he could always fall back on the rules and follow protocol exactly as he'd been trained to, but interacting with people in a non-professional capacity left him floundering and clueless.

Stella Rockley deserved much more than a simple *thank you* for the flowers and the card and the hospital visit. And he'd felt this was his chance to get to know her better, to talk to her, to.....be friends, maybe? He wanted so much more.

Bit he wouldn't even dare to hope for any more than friendship. She was so beautiful, so---way out of his league.

Feeling dejected, Chad walked into the station and was instantly besieged by warm greetings from his co-workers. They slapped him on the back, patted his shoulder, and rubbed his head like he was their favorite little brother.

For the first ten minutes, it seemed like '*Montague! Glad you're alive!*' and '*Good job, rookie*', was the running theme. It was overwhelming and left Chad humble and awkward and speechless once again.

His co-workers had just left him alone after the first few times he'd refused to hang out with them at the shooting range, for group barbecues after work or for deer hunting during hunting season.

He'd overheard them complain once, in the men's room, that he didn't know how to be a team player, and they weren't sure if he could be trusted to watch their backs when things got dangerous. It had devastated him. The one thing he prided himself on was utter loyalty to his co-workers, his job, his family.

Maybe, Chad thought, as he made his way to his locker and his sports bag, maybe saving that little kid had earned him their trust and respect, even if he still didn't know how to hang out and smile and chat like the other guys. Maybe all they wanted was to know that they could trust him with their lives when things got tough. Maybe that was enough? If so, it was worth getting shot for.

Chad closed his eyes. When Ames's bullet had grazed him in the neck, it had felt like a bee sting at first. Chad had ignored it and fired back.

As he watched Ames choke on his own blood from a punctured lung, he felt the warm liquid gushing out from his own neck. It was only then that he felt the pain like someone was touching a hot poker to his neck.

He fell to the ground, clutching at the wound. The thought came to him then as he lay there in that bullet-ridden entryway: *I'm going to die. I'm going to die, and I never got to tell her.....*

7

———

The couple at booth number four were so sweet together it made Stella's teeth ache. They sat across from each other, their hands linked on top of the table while they browsed through the menu. Both of them wore shiny new matching wedding rings.

"Are you ready to order?" Stella looked between them.

The woman looked up. "I think we are." She looked across to where the man was still browsing through the menu, fingers stroking an invisible beard. "Stop that," she playfully slapped his hand away from his chin.

"What? I miss it," he said, laughing.

"He had this full caveman beard, you see," the woman said, looking up at Stella.

"Did he?" Stella said, just to be polite. For some reason she really wasn't in the mood to watch these two— newly-weds — act all lovey-dovey.

"Yeah, but she didn't like it," the man chimed in. "Kept complaining about how it was irritating her skin, if you know what I mean." He had a mischievous grin.

Stella was squeezing her order pad so hard the wire binding started to bend out of shape.

"Shut up, sweetie!" The woman giggled and slapped him on the arm. "That's private information!"

Stella tried not to think of Chad appearing at The Truckstop completely clean shaven.

"He'd been wearing a beard for so long," the woman said, giving him a melting look. "But he shaved it all off the moment I asked him to."

"Of course," the man said, bringing his new wife's hand up to kiss the back of it. "I'd do anything for you, darlin'."

"Okay, that's it!" Stella took her apron off. "I'm sorry, but there's this guy, and I have to make a phone call. Right now."

A knowing look passed over the woman's face. "Go for it! Of course, of course! Go for it."

"Someone else will take your order," Stella called out over her shoulder.

"I need to make a phone call," she snapped at Jamie.

"Finally," Jamie said as she stomped through the kitchen and out the back door. "Finally, you're maybe gonna take a chance on him? It's about time, Stella Mia."

She glared at him and slammed out the kitchen door.

Out by the dumpsters, Stella fished out her phone and found his phone number right away. She bit her lip and shuffled her feet, her thumb hovering on the green *call* button. She closed her eyes, muttered a prayer, and pressed it.

Chad was driving to the gym when his cell rang. His heart thumped when he saw Stella's name on the display, and he carefully pulled to the side of the road.

"Constable—Chad," she began. "I wanted---"And then she stopped, and the silence stretched like thin elastic.

He knew it was now or never. "Stella, I'm sorry I left the

way I did. There was so much more I wanted to say. I'm a hopeless dolt at conversation."

She made a small sound in her throat. He hoped she wasn't laughing.

She wasn't laughing, was she? But he could tell by the softness of her tone that she wasn't when she said, "Why—why don't you come back and we'll start all over again?"

He'd hung up and turned the car around before he realized he hadn't said he was on his way.

He didn't burst through the door this time. Instead, he opened it hesitantly and stepped slowly into the diner.

Stella was cleaning a table. She turned around and looked at him, dishrag hanging from her hand.

"Have a seat somewhere," Jamie said from the front counter, pouring steaming hot coffee into two mugs. "You can go on your break, Stella." He gave her a huge, suggestive wink. "I've got this. Take as long as you want. Just talk loud enough so I can hear."

She was going to kill Jamie, first chance she had.

Suddenly remembering that they were still standing awkwardly in the middle of the diner, Stella looked around and picked booth number seven, by the south-facing window, the furthest away from the kitchen.

Chad followed her lead and slid into the seat across from her.

Jamie hurried over with two cups of coffee and winked at Chad as he turned away. "You got this, my man. Just say what's in your heart."

Stella picked up her cup and took a sip instead of throwing it at Jamie. She was grateful to have something for her hands to do. She tried not to stare too much as she watched him fiddle with the rim of the saucer. He had nice big hands, long fingers, clean short cut nails. She'd seen him do something similar with the brim of his hat before, fiddle with it like this. It must be a quirk of his or a nervous habit.

If *he* was nervous, she had him beat by a country mile.

"They told me you came to the hospital right away," he finally said, his gaze fixed on the tabletop as if the fake marble design was something he had suddenly found himself intensely interested in. "And I just want to say," he looked up, and she met his lovely brown eyes. "Thank you, for caring. For coming. For the flowers."

Stella put her coffee cup down. "You're welcome," she said. For some reason, she hadn't really expected him to actually come out and say those words: *thank you for caring.* It just didn't seem like something he would do. But what did she really know about him? Well, no time like the present.

"Did you always—"

"Where did you—"

"What made you—"

"I want to—"

They both stopped talking.

"You first, Constable—ummm, Chad," she said, stirring the coffee hard with a spoon, even though she took it black.

"So where did you grow up, Stella?"

It wasn't what she thought he'd say, turning the tables neatly on her. But it was okay.

"Vancouver. And no, I don't miss it one tiny bit."

"You have family there?"

"Just my mother. We don't get along."

"Why's that?"

Whoa. Once he got going, this guy actually knew how to talk. Her experience with men was that they usually preferred to talk about themselves, not listen to her. And he was *really* listening.

She'd always avoided being honest about her mother,

about her life. But now, the truth just came out. "She wants me to live out her dreams for her. And I don't want to."

He nodded and studied her face, his gaze going from her lips to her nose to her eyes. He didn't look away, and she didn't either. It almost hurt, the depth of interest and caring she saw in his eyes.

"What dreams, Stella? What did she want for you? What do *you* want for you?"

He had the most beautiful eyes. Nobody ever asked what she wanted for herself. It made her shy. But she wanted him to know.

She usually didn't tell people about the modelling. They tended to get the wrong impression, like she was some star or something, or else that she was a dumb bimbo who could only capitalize on her looks.

Either way, it embarrassed her. But she blurted it out anyway. It had taken her a long time to make sense of it.

"Candace is a single mom, she raised me on her own. My dad deserted us when he found out she was pregnant. I have no idea where he is, I've never met him. Anyhow, she started me modelling when I was three."

"Wow. That's really young to start working."

"It sure was." Her heart hurt when she remembered being so little, wanting so badly to please her mother, to make her love her. Hating the hot, bright lights, the men who told her to turn this way and that, to smile. Always to smile.

"By the time I was fourteen, she'd signed me with an agency that wanted me to travel, London, Paris, Milan. I was *so* done with the whole modelling thing. But she could sign the contracts on my behalf, and she did. So off we went."

"And how was that?" His full attention was on her. It was disconcerting and flattering. It made her want to hug him.

"Awful. We lived in one tiny room after another, and I was working most of the time so we didn't really explore Europe. Candace had it in her head that I should meet and marry some European billionaire, which I found ridiculous and laughable. But she got us invited to parties, which I hated." Far from wanting to marry her, most of the rich creeps wanted just to go to bed with her.

"Candace still does think that way. Anyway, when I turned eighteen, I took control, turned down all the gigs, came home to Vancouver and started waitressing. And from then on, living at home was hell. *She* wanted to travel, I had no desire to go anywhere. We still fight over it. I try to talk to her, but she just rants about me wasting my life, wasting my opportunities, and then she hangs up on me."

"But you stay in touch?"

"Yeah. She always knows where I am." She wouldn't tell him the worst part. It was too awful. Instead, she said, "I was tempted not to even tell her where I was living this time, but I couldn't do that to her. I'm all she has." And the phone calls came regularly, just as always, usually in the middle of the night. "At least she can't just turn up at my apartment or at The Truckstop."

He nodded. "Vancouver's quite a distance from Starwood."

"Thank heaven for that. Candice might want to travel, but a coal mining town in the Rockies isn't her idea of luxury, thank goodness." Stella gave a little laugh, but it came out sad instead of happy.

He reached over and patted her hand. "So what about you? What do *you* really want out of life, Stella?"

She smiled at him, aware of his touch. "You really ask tough questions, don't you?"

"I'm not much for small talk. Besides, how else do two people get to know each other?"

"True." She had to think for a couple minutes. She hadn't told anyone about her plans, just in case they didn't work out. She realized that in her own way, she was as reticent as Chad had always seemed. She'd learned early never to confide in Candace, and the habit had become ingrained.

What *did* she truly want? She sipped her coffee. "It's pretty simple, really." She took a deep breath and let it out on a sigh. "I'd like to train as a paramedic. I've been saving all my money, I'd have to go to Calgary to train. I've got an application, I just haven't filled it out."

Wow. It made it seem *almost* possible when she actually said it out loud.

"That's great, Stella. Would you get on with the Ambulance Service here in Starwood? Or move to a larger center?" He looked a bit anxious.

"I'd stay here. I really like it here."

"Me too." Was that relief in his voice? "Starwood's a great little town."

She turned the tables on him. "How about you---ummmm, Chad? Where did you grow up?"

"In Saskatchewan, city of Saskatoon. My dad and two older brothers are both in the police force. One brother, Griffin, is stationed in Calgary. Dad is in Ottawa, Oliver is in Toronto."

"Are your brothers married?"

He nodded. "I even have two nephews, little guys, one belonging to each brother. My bro's are both older than I am."

"How old is that?" She'd always wondered. He looked so young, which was part of why that ridiculous mustache had been—ridiculous.

"I'll be 30 in April."

Good, older than her. She'd been a little concerned. "Hey, my birthday's in April too. What date is yours?"

"April 5th."

"Get out of here. Mine is April 6th."

They stared at one another. Recognition dawned, and he looked horrified.

"That was the day—" he began.

Stella nodded. "Yup. The day you pulled me over. The day you fined me practically every last cent I had. Not the best birthday I've ever had." Somehow it didn't matter as much now.

He ducked his head, his face turning magenta. "I am *so* sorry for that, Stella. You don't know how many times I've wanted to apologize for that night. And it was your birthday, too. Is—is there any way I could make it up to you?"

Here it was. Did she have the courage to flirt with him again?

"Dinner would be nice. Just not here at the Truckstop." All she needed was Jamie giving her the fish eye the entire time. Just as he was right now. She caught the vigorous wave he gave her and she glowered at him. Fortunately, Chad didn't see.

"Would you—do you want to go to Fernie, Stella, or would you maybe consider letting me cook for you? I'm a good cook." He looked so eager, so excited at the prospect. "Growing up with my dad and brothers, somebody had to learn, or we'd all have starved."

"That—wow, that would be really nice. I have to tell you, I can't boil water without burning it. That's one of the reasons I love this job, Jamie feeds me."

He also got on her last nerve, but that would wait for another time.

"How does tomorrow night sound? I'm on leave for a while, so lots of free time."

"That sounds wonderful."

"I live in the Valleyview apartments, number 19. Six o'clock okay?"

Stella was working tomorrow. But she could maybe get Madison, the other waitress, to cover for her for the dinner rush. Madison owed her; Stella had taken the other woman's shifts when she'd dumped her Harley last month and wrecked her leg.

"Sure. Six it is."

He looked as if a light bulb had gone on inside him. His eyes smiled at her, and he leaned across and took her hand in his.

His fingers curled around hers, and it felt good.

"You won't be sorry, Stella. I'll make you the best meal ever. I promise."

He was so earnest, so intense. She couldn't wait for Saturday night.

8

———

The following afternoon Stella spent more time than usual figuring out what to wear.

Madison had been happy to take the entire afternoon shift, so Stella had time for a leisurely bath in Blanche's big bathroom at the B&B. She re-colored her hair, making it a brighter pink. Then she examined her closet. She really was short on anything resembling dress up. But then, she didn't want to make Chad uncomfortable by getting too fancy, either.

She finally settled on a short denim skirt and a plain white tee. At the last moment she added a bright pink hat and her heart-shaped sunglasses. They were rose-colored; they helped her see the world in its best light. She so wanted tonight to work.

The delicious smells wafted out the moment Chad opened the door.

"Stella, come in, make yourself at home. Would you like some wine? Or beer, I have lots of different kinds of beer. Or a wine cooler, I have lots of different kinds of coolers? Or rum, or Scotch, or----"

She had to giggle. "What did you do, buy out the liquor store?"

"Not quite." He was adorably serious and flushed, a towel tied around his middle over what looked like ironed blue jeans. He was also wearing a crisp white shirt. Fortunately, he'd skipped the tie. "I didn't think to ask what you'd like to drink."

"I'm not much of a drinker, but white wine would be lovely, thanks." She was looking around at his apartment. One entire wall was bookshelves. She went closer to examine the titles.

"You love mysteries," she said. "And poetry, you actually read poetry?"

It was the last thing she'd have guessed about him. And give him credit, he wasn't the least bit embarrassed.

"Some of those were my mother's," he said, handing Stella a wine glass. "She used to read me poetry when I was little. So I just went on reading it after she died."

Stella had never read poetry just for fun. She hadn't understood it in school. "Can you tell me some?"

"Poetry?"

"Yeah. Tell me some."

He thought for a moment, looked suddenly shy, and then said,

"Jenny kissed me when we met,
Jumping from the chair she sat in,
Time, you thief, who love to get,
Sweets into your list, put that in."

"Wow. That's so romantic, Chad."

He turned red. She loved that he blushed.

His apartment was small, but he'd made it homey. Plants lined the windowsill in the tiny kitchen, bright framed prints hung on the walls of the living room. On a small table was a photo of him and his family. Four men, standing stiff and straight, all in RCMP red serge. She picked it up and studied it, and he pointed at the uniformed men.

"That's Griffin. This is Oliver. That's my dad."

"Good looking guys." There was a strong family resemblance. Chad was the shortest, but in her opinion, he was also the cutest. He was so lucky, to have such a normal family. "Really handsome guys."

"Yeah. I sort of missed that gene."

"Get over yourself. You're not half bad, Constable Chad Montague."

He gave her that shy smile. She was so glad he'd shaved off the mustache.

"I'd like to have you meet my family, Stella. They'd love you."

She thought about her mother's reaction if Candace found out Stella was interested in a small-town cop. She shuddered. It wouldn't be pretty.

"Come and sit down. Dinner is ready. Would you like some more wine?"

He poured it, and she sat. He'd put music on, something soft and evocative. He had a water glass with wild roses in the center of the table. He went into the kitchen and came back with a salad, beautifully grilled local salmon and tiny potatoes.

"Ohhhh, yum. You really *can* cook." She'd sort of been expecting Kraft's Mac and Cheese. She loaded her plate.

He sat, lifted his wineglass and saluted her.

"To you, beautiful Stella."

It was her turn to blush.

They ate, chatting easily about people they both knew, situations Chad had found himself in, and weird customers Stella had encountered.

They laughed together. He *did* have a sense of humor, Stella realized. It just wasn't always obvious.

After dinner, she helped him clean up. They were standing side by side at the sink, him washing, her drying. He'd rolled up his shirt sleeves. His muscular forearms were covered in short golden hair, and for some reason, she couldn't take her eyes off of them.

He handed her a plate. He had soap bubbles on his cheek, and she set the plate down and brushed them away with her fingertips. Then she leaned in and put her lips on his.

There was no hesitation; she'd been wanting to kiss him since she walked in the door. His arms, soap and all, came around her, drawing her close. He smelled delicious, like soap and spices and healthy man. And oh my goodness, the man could kiss.

Stella melted into him, her entire body humming with pleasure, and things were just getting really interesting when her cell phone began its irritating warble.

She ignored it, but it just stopped and then began all over again.

"Shoot!" She moved just far enough away from Chad to retrieve the darned thing from her skirt pocket.

The display showed Jamie.

"What!" she snapped, wanting to smack the annoying man upside the ear hole. "Can't I have a single afternoon free without you----"

Jamie interrupted her, and there wasn't even the faintest tease in his voice. "Stella, your mother is here. At the Truckstop. She drove up in an old Chevy, nearly came through our front window. She's had way too much to drink, she's insisting on seeing you, and she's totally out of control, insulting the customers and staggering around.

Either you come and handle her or I'll have to call the cops."

"I'll—I'll be right there." Despair and rage and keen disappointment rolled through her in waves. She pulled away from Chad and went looking for wherever she'd left her handbag. "I have to go, Chad. Something's—something's come up and I have to go. Thank you for—"

"Whoa. Hold on a minute. What's going on, Stella?"

She looked at him, and all she could see was her chance of happiness draining away like the dishwater in the sink. Tears clogged her throat, and she had to struggle hard to control them. "My--my mother's turned up at the Truckstop. She's making a scene, I have to go and deal with it."

"Okay, we'll take my car." He reached for her hand.

She shook free. "I'm going alone, Chad. You don't understand. You have no idea how ugly this can get. I don't want you part of it."

He took both her arms in his hands, and he was strong.

She couldn't pull away. She stood still for an instant, staring into his dear face, his beautiful eyes, that sexy mouth, and it felt as if her heart was breaking.

"Everyone knows you here, Chad. You have your career to consider. I don't want you embarrassed by me or by her."

She drew a shaky breath. She had to tell him, he'd find out anyway. "Candace is an alcoholic. When she's drinking, she's ugly and mean. She's lost me more jobs by turning up at my work and causing an awful scene. She's doing that right now. She nearly drove in through the front window of the Truckstop, she's insulting customers, and Jamie's gonna call the cops if I don't go and get her out of there."

He just nodded. "That's really rough, Stella. I have an uncle who's an alcoholic, my mother's brother. He's gone thru every possible rehab unit, and when he gets out he goes straight back to boozing."

"I've tried to get Candace into rehab, but it doesn't work. She needs to want to get better, and she doesn't." Tears welled in her eyes. "I really hoped she wouldn't follow me here. I'd hoped---"

She'd hoped for a chance to really get to know this man. She was half in love with him, had been for a very long time. Well, she'd simply have to get over it.

Somehow.

"I need to go, Chad. Thank you so much for the dinner, I had a great time." She was trying not to give in to the tears that burned just behind her eyes. "You're a marvellous cook."

He shook his head and held on to her. "You're not going anywhere without me. I haven't had a chance to tell you this. I was planning on doing it at a better time. See, I'm in love with you, Stella. I know it's too soon, I know you don't have the same feelings for me. I know we need to see a lot more of each other, get to know one another better. But if you think a little thing like your mother being drunk and disorderly will change how I feel, you really don't know me. I'm good with people who are drunk and disorderly."

She'd have to trust him a whole lot to let him see Candace at her worst.

She had big issues with trust. It had never worked out for her in the past, trusting anyone. The last guy she'd trusted had ransacked her purse. And women—well, her mother had been an object lesson there. How many times had Stella believed her when she promised to stop drinking?

She heard Jamie's annoying voice in her head. *"Finally, you're gonna take a chance on him?"*

Maybe Jamie was right. Maybe it was time to take some chances.

"Let's take your car," she said.

*****

AFTERWORD

Bobby says:

I was born and grew up in this little Rocky Mountain coal mining town of Sparwood, B.C., Canada. Our big claim to fame is THE BIG TRUCK, advertised as the world's largest, parked on a lot right when you come into town.

I always wanted to start a restaurant near it and call it the Biggest Little Truckstop In The World.

Well, we all know what the failure rate is with restaurants, so instead, I decided to write a series of romances about an imaginary town called Starwood.

Here's a picture of the truck, thanks to my sister Karen.

That's me in the white jacket down by the wheel.

ALSO BY BOBBY HUTCHINSON

STARWOOD CHRONICLES

Biggest Little Truckstop

Every Little Thing

Biggest Little Mustache

Biggest Little Heart

Biggest Little Secret

MEDICAL ROMANCE

Drastic Measures

Full Recovery

Double Jeopardy

Picking Clover,

Nursing the Doctor

Patient Care

The Baby Doctor

Acute Care

A Past And Present Love

Love To The Rescue

One Little Miracle

Healer

WESTERN PRAIRIE BRIDES

(Historical Romance)

Lantern In The Window

Silent Light, Silent Love

Medicine Woman

Rose's Maile Order Brides And Grooms

Darling Clementine

Tangled Lives

ABOUT THE AUTHOR

Bobby Hutchinson lives, breathes, reads and writes books. She lives in a small city in the Rocky Mountains of B.C., Canada, a little larger version of Starwood.

She isn't an RCMP officer, she doesn't waitress anymore, she's never shot a stalker-but some of her wonderful female friends have done (most) of the above, which made for fantastic research in Biggest Little Mustache.

Her favorite quote is, "When you change the way you look at a thing, the thing you look at changes."

Copyright © 2018 by Bobby Hutchinson

All rights reserved.

No part of this book may be reproduced in any form or by any electronic or mechanical means, including information storage and retrieval systems, without written permission from the author, except for the use of brief quotations in a book review.

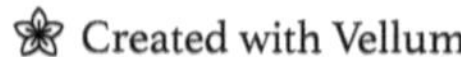 Created with Vellum

www.ingramcontent.com/pod-product-compliance
Lightning Source LLC
Chambersburg PA
CBHW021758150726

47989CB00004B/1709